Mr. Harrison Is Embarrassin'!

Dan Gutman

Pictures by
Jim Paillot

HARPER
An Imprint of HarperCollins Publishers

To Nathaniel Lewis

Library of Congress Cataloging-in-Publication Data is available.
ISBN 978-0-06-196919-5 (lib. bdg.) — ISBN 978-0-06-196918-8 (pbk.)

Typography by Joel Tippie
11 12 13 14 15   CG/BR   10 9 8 7 6 5 4
❖
First Edition

Contents

School for Cavemen

My name is A.J. and I hate coffee.

I *do!* Did you ever taste coffee? I tried it once and I thought I was gonna throw up.

My parents drink coffee every day with breakfast. What's up with that?

"If I don't get my cup of coffee in the morning," my dad said, "I'm a mess."

"How can you drink that stuff?" I asked him. "It tastes like dirt."

"Well, it was just ground this morning," he replied. And then he slapped his knee and bent over laughing even though he didn't say anything funny.*

I was thinking about it. There must be some chemical in the brain that gets activated when you become a grown-up. Then, suddenly, you start to drink coffee, eat vegetables, wear a tie, and go to craft fairs. There's no other way to explain why grown-ups willingly do any of that stuff.

I was walking to school with my friends

---

*That's a grown-up joke that isn't funny to kids—sort of like those dog whistles that humans can't hear.

Ryan, Michael, and Neil, who we call the nude kid even though he wears clothes. These annoying girls—Andrea, Emily, and Alexia—were behind us as we climbed up the front steps. That's when I saw this big sign . . .

HAPPY BiRtHdaY ELLa MeNtRY SchooL!
50 Years of Teaching stuff

"Wow, I didn't know it was the school's birthday," said Michael, who never ties his shoes.

"We should give the school a party," said Ryan, who will eat anything, even stuff that isn't food.

"Schools don't get birthday parties," said Andrea, rolling her eyes. "They're not people."

"That's right," said Emily, who always agrees with everything Andrea says.

"Fifty years!" Alexia said. "That's a *long* time!"

"Yeah," I told everybody, "when the school first opened, the students were probably cavemen."

"I'll bet they taught the kids reading, writing, and how to start a fire by rubbing two sticks together," said Neil.

"And they didn't have to learn history back then," Ryan said, "because nothing happened yet!"

Me and the guys laughed and high-fived each other. It was hilarious.

"Boys!" Andrea said, rolling her eyes again.

"Hey," said Alexia, "back in those days, instead of buses, kids probably rode to school on dinosaurs."

I laughed and high-fived Alexia. She is pretty cool even though she's a girl.

Andrea put on her mean face.

"The dinosaurs died *millions* of years ago, Alexia!" she said. "That was long before there were people."

"Can you possibly be any more boring?" Alexia asked Andrea.

Wow! That's what *I* was going to say!

Andrea gave Alexia another mean face.

Michael pulled open the front door of the school. That's when we saw the strangest thing in the history of the world.

But I'm not going to tell you what it was.

Okay, okay, I'll tell you.

The teachers were walking around like zombies! They all had their hands out in front of them and this dazed look in their eyes. Mr. Docker. Mrs. Cooney. Ms. Coco. Miss Holly. All of them! Some of the teachers were groaning, drooling, and bumping into the walls.

"What's the matter with the teachers?" Andrea asked.

"This must be Act Like a
Zombie Day," I said.

"Maybe they're filming a horror movie,"
suggested Ryan.

"Are you okay?" Emily asked Mrs.

MUST hAVE COFFEE...

Yonkers, the computer teacher, who was stumbling around like she was still asleep.

Mrs. Yonkers just stared back with creepy horror movie eyes.

"...must have coffee...," she muttered.

"...need coffee...," groaned Mr. Macky, the reading specialist.

"...will die without coffee...," mumbled Ms. Hannah, the art teacher.

Grown-ups are weird.

Night of the Living Teachers

All the teachers were stumbling around like it was a scene out of *Night of the Living Dead*. It was cool. We all went into the front office to see what was going on.

"What's going on?" I asked Mrs. Patty, the school secretary.

"Our coffee machine is on the fritz," she said.

"What's a fritz?" I asked. "And why would you put a coffee machine on one of them? Maybe they should take the coffee machine off the fritz and it would work again."

"On the fritz means something is *broken*, Arlo," Andrea said, rolling her eyes. She calls me by my real name because she knows I don't like it.

"Your *face* is on the fritz," I told Andrea.

"Fritz." That's a weird word.

Suddenly, our principal, Mr. Klutz, came rushing in from his office. He has no hair at all. I mean *none*. Mr. Klutz looked like

he would have been tearing his hair out,
if he had any hair.

"I don't know what to do," he said. "If
the teachers don't get their coffee in the
morning, we could have a disaster on our
hands!"

Teachers were wandering in and out of the office like monsters.

". . . must have coffee . . ."

". . . need coffee . . ."

". . . life is empty without coffee . . ."

". . . go to Starbucks . . ."

Boy, grown-ups sure do like coffee. What is their problem?

"We've got to *do* something!" shouted Emily, and she went running out of the office.

"Where's Miss Lazar?" asked Mr. Klutz. "She usually takes care of the coffee machine."

"It's her day off," said Mrs. Patty.

Miss Lazar is the school custodian.

Things always seem to go on the fritz when she has a day off.

I thought the teachers were going to start a riot or something. But you'll never believe who walked into the door at that moment.

Nobody. If you walked into a door, it would hurt. But you'll never believe who walked into the *doorway*.

It was Mr. Harrison, the tech guy at our school. He fixes computers and laser printers and copy machines. He is really skinny, and he has blond hair.

"Good morning, good morning!" Mr. Harrison said to everybody.

He was holding a paper coffee cup. I

guess he must have stopped off to buy coffee on the way to school. Some of the teachers saw his cup and surrounded him. ". . . must have coffee . . . ," groaned Miss Laney, the speech teacher.

Mr. Harrison leaned his head back to finish his coffee.

"Ah, that hit the spot," he said, throwing the cup in the garbage.

Miss Laney reached into the garbage can, grabbed the cup, and tried to lick a few drops of coffee from it.

"Maybe you can help us, Mr. Harrison," said Mr. Klutz. "The coffee machine is broken."

"Yeah, it needs to get off the fritz," I added.

"Can you fix it?" Mr. Klutz asked. "If we don't get some coffee soon, I'm afraid the teachers will be revolting."

"Some of the teachers are already revolting," I said.

"Leave it to me," said Mr. Harrison. "I can fix anything. They don't call me Fritz Harrison for nothing."

"Is Fritz *really* your name?" I asked.

"No, it's just my nickname."

"What's your real name?" I asked.

"Oh, I can't tell you that."

A bunch of teachers gathered around to watch while Mr. Harrison examined the coffee machine.

"It's simple, really," he said. "The water goes in this tube to the drip area. This switch sends electricity to a heating element, and blah blah blah sensors blah blah fuses to keep it from getting too hot blah blah blah one-way valve blah blah blah blah filtration system and blah blah blah . . ."

Mr. Harrison went on like that for a

million hundred minutes. He made it sound like the inside of a coffee machine was a rocket ship.

"So, do you know what's wrong with it?" asked Mr. Klutz.

"Sure," Mr. Harrison replied. "It's not plugged in."

He plugged in the coffee machine, and it started making coffee right away. The teachers cheered and clapped him on the back.

"Hooray for Mr. Harrison!" they yelled.

"He fixed the coffee machine!"

"He should get the Nobel Prize!"*

"He's our hero!"

---

*That's a prize they give out to people who don't have bells.

Big Nose

After the teachers got their coffee, everything was back to normal. Or as normal as things *ever* get at Ella Mentry School.

The bell rang, and we all rushed to Mr. Granite's class. We pledged the allegiance, did Word of the Day, and had circle time. That's when we all sit around in a circle, so it has the perfect name.

"Okay, turn to page twenty-three in your math books," said Mr. Granite.

We've been working on page twenty-three in our math books for a million hundred days. But every time we get started, there seems to be an interruption. That's fine with me, because math is boring.

"Today we're going to work on fractions," said Mr. Granite. "Now, which one of you can tell me—"

He didn't get the chance to finish his sentence because at that very moment an announcement came over the loud-speaker.

"Everyone, please report to the all-purpose room for an assembly," said Mrs. Patty.

"Yay!" me and the guys shouted. "No math!"

"What?!" Mr. Granite moaned. "Nobody told me we were having an assembly."

He was mad, but I was happy because we got out of math again. I didn't even mind that we had to walk a million hundred miles to the all-purpose room.

I got a seat next to Ryan, and Alexia sat on my other side. Andrea and that crybaby Emily were in front of us.

Mr. Klutz and our vice principal, Mrs. Jafee, got up on the stage. Mrs. Jafee made a peace sign with her fingers, which means "shut up."

"First of all, how about a big round of applause for Mr. Harrison?" said Mrs. Jafee. "He fixed the coffee machine."

Mr. Harrison took a bow. Everybody clapped in a circle and yelled "Hip hip hooray" until the teachers made the shut-up peace sign.

"Students, I have big news," announced Mr. Klutz.

"Mr. Klutz has a big nose," Alexia whispered in my ear.

Hey, that's what I was going to say!

"Today is Ella Mentry School's fiftieth birthday!" Mr. Klutz said.

"Hip hip hooray!" everybody yelled.*

"To help us celebrate, some special visitors are coming after lunch," Mr. Klutz told us. "Mayor Hubble is going to be here. A newspaper reporter. And Channel 7 News is even coming to film the celebration."

"Are we gonna be on TV?" some girl shouted.

"You betcha," said Mrs. Jafee.

"EEEEEEEEEK! We're gonna be on TV!"

All the girls started screaming and freaking out.

"We're gonna be famous!"

"It's going to be like a reality TV show!"

---

*What do hips have to do with cheering? That sounds like you're cheering for hips.

23

Girls are weird.

"How do I look?" asked Andrea. "I need to comb my hair."

"You look beautiful," said Emily. "How do I look?"

"You look beautiful, too," said Andrea.

"You both look ugly," I told them.

Mr. Klutz made the shut-up peace sign again.

"There will be one other special guest," he said. "Ella Mentry: the lady our school was named after. Just like our school is celebrating its birthday, so is Mrs. Mentry. She is ninety years old today, and she's going to celebrate right here with us. Isn't that exciting?"

"Yes!" said all the girls.

"No!" said all the boys.

"There's a reason why I called you all in here this morning," Mr. Klutz told us. "Do you kids remember what happened the *last* time Ella Mentry visited our school?"

How could I forget? It seemed like it was just yesterday. Our school had been named the cleanest school in the district, and Ella Mentry came to the vomitorium at lunchtime to give us the award.

The only problem was, I shot some peas and carrots up in the air with a spoon. They stuck to the ceiling for a few minutes, but then they landed on Andrea's head. So she dumped a bowl of spaghetti over

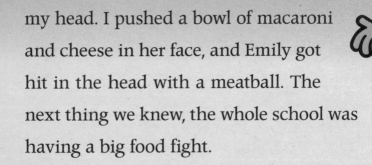

my head. I pushed a bowl of macaroni and cheese in her face, and Emily got hit in the head with a meatball. The next thing we knew, the whole school was having a big food fight.

That's when Ella Mentry showed up. She didn't give us the award for having the cleanest school in the district. But she did dump a bowl of chocolate pudding over Mr. Klutz's head.

"That was a very embarrassing day," said Mrs. Jafee. "We can't let it happen again. With the reporter and a camera crew coming, we need to show our school in the best possible light."

"You're going to shine lights on the school?" I asked.

Andrea turned around to roll her eyes at me.

"That means we need to be on our best behavior, Arlo," she whispered. "You should try it sometime."

"Oh, snap!" said Ryan.

"Mrs. Mentry doesn't like it when things

get dirty," Mr. Klutz told us. "So let's spend the rest of the morning cleaning up the school. I want this place to be as clean as a whistle when she arrives."

"Whistles aren't clean," I said to Alexia.

"Yeah," she replied. "Whistles are filled with people's spit. They're gross."

Andrea rolled her eyes at us.

"Clean as a whistle is an idiom," she said.

"*You're* an idiom," I told Andrea.

"Oh, snap!" said Ryan.

I had no idea what an idiom was, but it was just one letter away from "idiot," so I figured it was something mean that I could say to Andrea.

On the Fritz

We marched back to our class in single file. I was the line leader. Mr. Granite couldn't go back to our math lesson because we had to clean up the room for Ella Mentry. He gave each of us a rag and a spray bottle filled with water. Andrea started singing "The Clean-up Song" . . .

Clean up! Clean up!
Everybody everywhere!
Clean up! Clean up!
Everybody do your share.

Except that me and the guys changed the last line to "Even in your underwear."

It was hilarious. Anything to do with underwear is hilarious.

Andrea thinks cleaning is fun. What is her problem? Cleaning isn't fun. Getting dirty is fun. That's the first rule of being a kid.

But we did want everything to be perfect for when Mrs. Mentry and the news reporter showed up. I was cleaning off the computer table in the corner when I noticed that the screen was filled with a bunch of strange numbers and letters that made no sense at all.

"Mr. Granite, the computer is on the

fritz," I said.

"Maybe I can fix it," said Andrea. "I take a computer class after school."

Andrea takes classes in *everything* after school. If they gave a class in how to take classes, she would take that class so she could get better at class taking.

As it turned out, Andrea couldn't fix the computer. Mr. Granite had to call Mr. Harrison on the intercom. He came running in a few minutes later.

"Your computer is on the fritz?" Mr. Harrison asked.

"It was working fine just yesterday," Mr. Granite told him.

"Can you get it off the fritz?" I asked.

Mr. Harrison removed the back of the computer and started poking around at the insides with a screwdriver.

"I see what's going on here," he said. "Your external parallel processor can't access enough gigaflops to bitmap the binary protocol blah blah blah blah blah. All we need is to upload a new firewall so the network can reboot your motherboard and maximize the serial bandwidth blah blah blah blah blah."

Mr. Harrison talks funny. Nobody had any idea what he was saying. But in a minute or two, the computer was working fine.

"Hip hip hooray!" I cheered. "The computer is off the fritz!"

"While you're here," said Mr. Granite, "our SMART Board went on the fritz yesterday."

"Yeah," I said, "that thing is busted. It should be called a dumb board."

"Can you fix it?" asked Mr. Granite.

"No problem," said Mr. Harrison. "I just need to debug the analog Bluetooth vector blah blah blah blah blah blah . . ."

Nobody had any idea what he was talking about. But of course, a few seconds later, the SMART Board was off the fritz.

Mr. Harrison can fix *anything*: computers, laser printers, scanners, intercoms, microphones, even pencil sharpeners and coffee machines. And there's plenty of old, broken-down stuff to fix at our school.

That's the thing about a fifty-year-old school. Everything is always on the fritz and falling apart. One time, a piece of plaster fell off the ceiling in the hallway and hit Emily in the head. It was a real Kodak moment. We need to have a tech guy all the time just to fix the stuff that breaks.

"Hip hip hooray!" we all yelled when Mr. Harrison turned on the SMART Board.

"I'm just doing my job," he said. "When I see something is broken, I want to fix it."

"Can you fix Andrea's brain?" I asked. "Because it's broken."

"Oh, snap!" said Ryan.

Andrea was going to say something mean to me, but she couldn't because there was an announcement over the loudspeaker.

"Mr. Harrison, please report to the office. The copy machine is on the fritz again."

Mr. Harrison sighed.

"I just fixed that old thing yesterday," he told us. "It's worn-out. I don't think I can fix it again. I'll just have to build a new copy machine like the old one."

"So you're going to make a copy of the copy machine?" I asked.

"That's right."

No, that's weird.

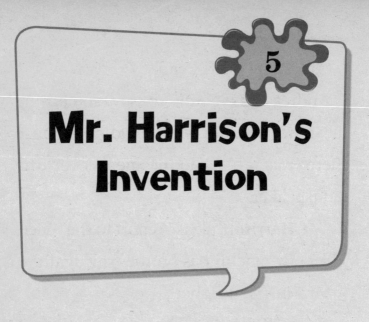

Mr. Harrison's Invention

5

I was in the vomitorium eating lunch at a table with the guys and Alexia. Andrea and her girlie girl friends were at the next table.

"What do you think Mr. Harrison's real name is?" Alexia asked as she bit into a peanut butter sandwich.

"He told us his name is Fritz," said Ryan, who was eating a salad. Ryan will eat anything, even stuff that grew in the dirt.

"Fritz is Mr. Harrison's *nickname*," Andrea said. "He won't tell us his real name."

"It must be really weird," Michael said. "If he had a normal name, he would tell us what it was."

"His name is probably Poindexter," said Neil the nude kid, "or Dorkus."

"We need to find out his real name," I said. "He may be an impostor."

"What?" Emily asked. She looked all scared, like always.

"Maybe Mr. Harrison isn't a real tech guy at all," I explained. "Did you ever think of that? Maybe he kidnapped our tech guy."

"Stop trying to scare Emily," said Andrea.

"I'm scared!" said Emily.

"He probably took a laser out of one of the laser printers," I said, "and he's shooting laser beams at the real tech guy right *now*."

"We've got to *do* something!" said Emily, and then she went running out of the vomitorium. That girl will fall for anything.

Emily didn't have to go anywhere. Because you'll never believe who walked into the vomitorium at that moment.

It was Mr. Harrison! And he was holding an umbrella.

"How do you like my new invention?"

he asked us.

"You invented the umbrella?" asked Ryan.

"Oh, this isn't just *any* old umbrella," Mr. Harrison said. "It's a *solar-powered* umbrella."

"What?" Neil said. "I never heard of anything like that."

"See?" Mr. Harrison told us. "This umbrella has a built-in solar panel. It uses the power of the sun to open it. I've been working on it for years."

He pushed a button on the handle, and the umbrella opened up.

"WOW," we all said, which is "MOM" upside down.

"That's neat, Mr. Harrison!" said Andrea, who never misses the chance to brown-nose a grown-up.

"Wait a minute," I said. "Why would you need that? Nobody uses an umbrella when the sun is out. We only use an umbrella when it's raining."

"Hmmm," said Mr. Harrison, "you're right. It was a dumb idea."

Then he threw his solar-powered umbrella into the garbage can.

"I guess I should forget about the other invention I'm working on," he said, "a solar-powered flashlight."

Mr. Harrison must have been pretty mad that I didn't like his invention, because he stormed away. But as he turned around to leave, you'll never believe what happened.

He slipped on some spilled juice and fell down!

And when he fell down, you'll never believe what happened.

His wallet fell out of his pocket!

And when his wallet fell out of his pocket, you'll never believe what happened.

I pounced on it!

And when I pounced on the wallet, I opened it up and looked at the name on the driver's license. And you'll never believe what Mr. Harrison's first name is.

I'm not going to tell you.

Okay, okay, I'll tell you. But you have to read the next chapter. So nah-nah-nah boo-boo on you!

6

The Truth About Mr. Harrison

Mr. Harrison's first name is George.

"I know Mr. Harrison's real name," I told everybody after I handed back the wallet and he left.

"What is it?" Ryan asked.

"His name is . . . ," I said. "I'm not telling."

"Come on, A.J.!" said Michael. "Spill the beans."*

"I'll be your best friend," said Neil the nude kid.

"Arlo, what's Mr. Harrison's first name?" said Andrea.

"It's George," I said.

"George?" said Alexia. "That's not a weird name."

"I wonder why he wouldn't tell us his name was George," said Michael.

"George Harrison," said Andrea. "Wait a minute! George Harrison was somebody famous! He was one of the Beatles!"

"One of the *what*?" asked Neil the nude kid.

---

*What do beans have to do with anything?

"That old rock group, dumbhead," said Michael.

Oh, yeah! My parents told me about the Beatles, and I played this video game called Rock Band, where you play Beatle

songs. It's cool. Everybody knows who the Beatles were.

"Mr. Harrison was one of the Beatles?" asked Ryan.

"Wait a minute," Andrea said. "George Harrison of the Beatles died a long time ago."

"He must have faked his death," I told her. "Famous people do that all the time, you know."

"That doesn't make any sense, A.J.," said Michael. "Why would a big rock star fake his death and get a job as a tech guy in a school?"

"He probably hated being famous," I told them. "Celebrities get sick of signing autographs and having people take pictures of them all the time. He must be hiding out in our school so his fans won't bother him."

"Being a nerdy tech guy *would* be the perfect disguise," Alexia admitted.

"But Mr. Harrison doesn't look *anything* like the other George Harrison," Andrea said. "I've seen pictures of him."

"Haven't you ever heard of plastic surgery?" I asked her. "And he obviously dyed his hair blond so he would look completely different."

"He did not."

"Did too."

We went back and forth like that for a

while. But guess who came back into the vomitorium at that moment.

It was Mr. Harrison.

"It's time for the big birthday celebration!" he said, all excited. "If you want some cake, you need to go to the all-purpose room right away."

I love cake! I was about to run out of the vomitorium, but Mr. Harrison grabbed me.

"Whoa! Not so fast, A.J.," he said. "It's slippery in here. You might fall down and get hurt. I want to hold your hand."

WHAT?!

I looked at Alexia. Alexia looked at Ryan. Ryan looked at Michael. Michael looked at

Neil. Neil looked at Andrea.

And we all mouthed the same words.

"I want to hold your hand?"

See? I *told* you that Mr. Harrison was one of the Beatles!

The Weirdest Thing in the History of the World

We wanted to ask Mr. Harrison if he was one of the Beatles, but there was no time. We had to rush to the all-purpose room for the big birthday celebration. I was right behind Alexia.

When we got there, a giant cake was on

the stage. I mean *giant!* There must have
been enough cake for everybody in the
whole school to have a piece. And it was

covered with candles. I guess there were ninety of them, for Ella Mentry's birthday. Mr. Harrison went up onstage and started lighting them.

I saw Mayor Hubble talking to Mr. Klutz at the front of the room. Some guys were carrying around a big TV camera. I didn't see Ella Mentry anywhere.

Before we could sit down, a lady I never saw before grabbed me by the arm. She was wearing a hat that said PRESS on it, and she pulled out a pad and a pen.

"My name is Mrs. Lilly," she said. "I work for the *News Tribune Bulletin Inquirer.* Can I ask you kids a few questions?"

"Sure," Alexia and I replied.

"So what's your name, young man?" Mrs. Lilly asked.

"My name is A.J. and I hate school," I told her.

"Hello, little girl," Mrs. Lilly said. "What's *your* name?"

"My name is A.J. and I hate school," said Alexia.

"Both of you are named A.J.?" Mrs. Lilly asked us.

"Yes."

"And both of you hate school?"

"Yes."

"Tell me why," she said. "I need to get a scoop for my paper."

"Why do you need a scoop?" I asked.

"Did your dog make a poop?"

"No, I mean I'm here to get the *real* story about Ella Mentry School," Mrs. Lilly said. "I want the story *behind* the story."

"Well, the teachers here are all crazy," Alexia told her.

"Is that so?" Mrs. Lilly said as she jotted down notes in her pad. "Tell me more."

"Our teacher, Mr. Granite, is from

another planet," I told her. "He built a spaceship powered by potatoes so he could go home, but a cow bumped into it and it crashed into the playground."

"Interesting!" said Mrs. Lilly, writing quickly on her pad.

"Hey, can we press on your hat?" Alexia asked Mrs. Lilly.

"Why do you want to press on my hat?"

"Because it says PRESS on it!" I told her. "Duh!"

Mrs. Lilly is silly. She wanted to ask us more questions, but Mr. Klutz made a peace sign, so everybody had to shut up.

"Take a seat, A.J.," he said.

"I can't," I said. "All the seats are screwed

to the floor."

"He means sit down," Alexia told me.

I knew that.

"Some people might say Ella Mentry School is old," Mr. Klutz announced into the microphone. "Some people say it's falling apart. Not me. Our school has character blah blah blah. And our school has history blah blah blah. And our school has blah blah blah blah blah blah."

Mr. Klutz's speech was really boring. Then Mayor Hubble got up to speak.

"Blah blah blah blah," he said. "Blah blah blah blah blah blah blah blah blah blah blah blah blah blah blah blah blah blah blah blah blah blah blah blah

blah blah blah blah."

I thought I was gonna die.

"And now I would like to introduce our honored guest of the day," the mayor said. "The namesake of Ella Mentry Elementary School, Mrs. . . . Ella . . . Mentry!"

Mrs. Mentry is really old, and she came toddling out on the stage with a cane. That lady is *tiny*. She was about the size of

R2-D2 in *Star Wars*. Mr. Klutz adjusted the microphone so Ella Mentry could reach it.

"I'm so happy your school was named after me," Mrs. Mentry told us. "Because when you get to be my age, you forget things. And if I ever forget my name, I know that all I need to do is walk down the street and see it in big letters on the side of your school."

We weren't sure if Ella Mentry was making a joke or not. Maybe she really *does* have to walk by our school to remember her name. We all laughed, just to be on the safe side.

"You say it's your birthday," Ella Mentry said. "It's my birthday, too!"

Everybody cheered. She went behind the giant birthday cake and started to sing "Happy Birthday." The whole school joined in. It was loud!

When the song was over, Mrs. Mentry started to blow out the candles. There were like a million hundred of them. I thought she was gonna pass out.

Ella Mentry was in the middle of blowing out the candles when the weirdest thing in the history of the world happened.

I'm not going to tell you what it was.

Okay, okay, I'll tell you.

All the lights went out!

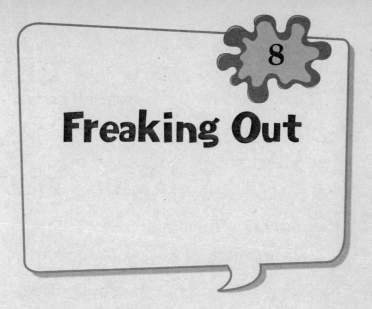

Freaking Out

Suddenly, we were all sitting there in the dark. The only light was coming from the candles on Ella Mentry's birthday cake. For a few seconds nobody knew what to do. It was scary!

"Everyone remain calm," said Mr. Klutz.

"The lights in the halls are out too,"

hollered Mr. Macky.

"The computers in the front office are down," shouted Mrs. Patty from the back of the all-purpose room.

"*Everything* is down," said one of the other teachers. "It's a total power failure."

"A blackout!" said Mayor Hubble. "Oh no! When the parents find out, they'll blame it on me, and I won't be reelected."

"Why is it that every time I come to visit your school, something bad happens?" asked Ella Mentry. "I've had enough of this!"

"I'm sure the lights will come back on any second, Mrs. Mentry," said Mr. Klutz.

"Let's not panic," said Mrs. Jafee.

"I'm afraid of the dark!" whined one of the first graders.

"I want my mommy!" yelled some other little kid.

Sheesh, get a grip! It was like the first graders had never been in the dark before. Those kids should take a chill pill.

The only problem was that as soon as one of those little first-grade munchkins starts in crying, all the rest of the first graders start in crying, too. And once all the first graders start in crying, the second graders start yelling and screaming. And once all the second graders start yelling and screaming, the third graders start freaking out.

"The world is coming to an end!" shouted Michael.

"Run for your life!" shouted Ryan.

"We're all going to die!" I shouted, just for the fun of it.

Mr. Klutz was probably making the shut-up peace sign with his fingers, but nobody could see it because it was too dark.

"Mrs. Mentry, are you okay?" Mr. Klutz shouted.

No reply.

"Mrs. Mentry?"

Silence. You could hear a pin drop in there.*

---

*That is, if there were any pins around. Which there weren't.

"Mrs. Mentry, where *are* you?" asked Mayor Hubble.

Nothing.

"Where's Mrs. Mentry?" yelled Mr. Klutz.

"Where's Mrs. Mentry?" yelled Mrs. Jafee.

"Where's Mrs. Mentry?" yelled Mr. Granite.

"Where's Mrs. Mentry?" everybody was yelling.

Mrs. Mentry was *gone*!

The Search Party

When all the kids realized that Ella Mentry was missing, they stopped crying and yelling and screaming and freaking out. Everybody was worried about Mrs. Mentry.

"I'm sure the lights will be back on any

moment and we'll find Mrs. Mentry," said Mr. Klutz. "For now I need everyone to stay calm."

Calm? Who can stay calm when all the lights are out and the ninety-year-old lady the school is named after has disappeared?

"Ella?" the teachers were all saying. "Where are you, Mrs. Mentry?"

"She was right here a minute ago," said Ms. Coco, the gifted and talented teacher. "I saw her standing there."

"Maybe she went to the bathroom," said Mr. Docker, the science teacher.

"Maybe she's hiding," suggested Mrs. Yonkers.

"Yoo-hoo!" said Miss Laney. "Mrs. Mentry? Come out, come out, wherever you are!"

"This is a tragedy!" said Mr. Klutz. "How do you lose a ninety-year-old lady?"

"She's pretty tiny," said Mrs. Jafee. "She could be anywhere."

"We *have* to find her," said Mayor Hubble. "If anything happens to Mrs. Mentry, the voters are going to blame me for it on Election Day."

All the grown-ups were upset. Well, all the grown-ups were upset except for one: that newspaper reporter, Mrs. Lilly.

"*Now* I have a story!" she said excitedly. "I can see the headline: EX-TEACHER ELLA

71

MENTRY VANISHES INTO THIN AIR! POLICE ARE BAFFLED! Finally, I'll have the scoop I've been waiting for my whole life!"

"Why don't you just go to a store and buy a scoop?" I asked.

Mr. Harrison lit all the candles on the cake again. Now we could see a little.

Ex-Teacher
Ella Mentry Vanishes
into thin Air!
Police Are Baffle

"Mr. Klutz," he said, "I think I know where Mrs. Mentry might be."

"Where?"

"She may have wandered down to the basement," Mr. Harrison said. "But to get to her, I'm going to need some little people."

"Why?" asked Mr. Klutz.

"I think she fell in a hole," said Mr. Harrison.

"She fell in a hole?" somebody yelled.

"She fell on a hoe?" somebody else yelled.

"She flew in a hotel?" somebody else yelled.

Everybody was yelling out all kinds of

crazy stuff that had nothing to do with falling in a hole.

"You say you need some little people," Mr. Klutz asked. "How little?"

"First graders and second graders might be too little," said Mr. Harrison. "Fourth and fifth graders might be too big. I need some third graders."

"I volunteer!" shouted Ryan, Michael, and Neil the nude kid.

"We do too!" said me and Alexia.

"I want to help find Mrs. Mentry too," said Andrea, who always wants to help grown-ups so they'll like her. Then, of course, Emily volunteered because she does everything that Andrea does.

"Good!" said Mr. Harrison. "Each of you come up here and take a piece of cake with a candle on it. We'll use the candles to light our way until the lights come back on. You won't see me."

"We get to have cake?" said Ryan, who is always thinking about eating. "Cool!"

"Follow me, kids," said Mr. Harrison.

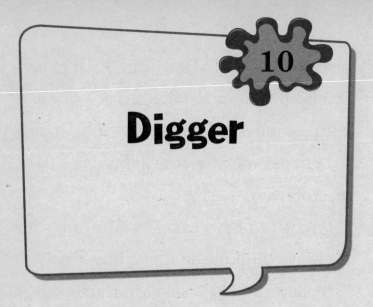

Digger

We each took a piece of cake with a candle stuck in it and followed Mr. Harrison down the stairs. I felt like a secret agent sneaking around in the dark. It was cool.

"Basements are scary," Emily said as we made our way downstairs.

"Yeah, there are probably monsters

down there," I told her.

"Stop trying to scare Emily," Andrea told me.

"I'm scared!" said Emily.

"Hey, can we eat this cake?" asked Ryan.

"You can't do that," said Mr. Harrison. "We need the candles to light our way."

"If we had solar-powered flashlights," I said, "we would be able to eat the cake."

"Well, you can't use your cake as a flashlight and eat it, too," said Mr. Harrison.

Finally, we reached the basement. At the bottom of the stairs, there was a hole in the floor. I almost fell in it.

"I noticed this hole yesterday," said Mr.

Harrison, "and I think I know who made it, too."

"Who?" we all asked.

"A squirrel."

"A squirrel?"

"A squirrel."*

Mr. Harrison told us that he had noticed a squirrel hanging around the monkey bars in the playground, digging deep holes in the dirt. He even gave her a name: Digger.

"I think Digger might have dug a hole into the school and chewed her way through an electrical wire," he told us. "That would knock out the power, and Mrs. Mentry might have fallen in the hole

_____

*Why is everyone saying "a squirrel"?

in the floor."

"WOW," we all said, which is "MOM" upside down.

"If Digger chewed through a live electrical wire," Mr. Harrison told us, "she probably got the shock of her life. There might be a fried squirrel down there."

"Ewwww, gross!" we all said.

"Poor Digger," said Emily.

"I wonder what fried squirrel tastes like," asked Ryan.

"Fried squirrel would have to be cooked in *oil*," Andrea said. "That's what 'fried' means. If Digger was electrocuted, she would have been broiled or baked. I take a cooking class after school, so I know these things."

Why can't an electrocuted squirrel fall on Andrea's head?

"Wait a minute!" said Alexia. "If Mrs. Mentry touches that live wire, she could get the shock of her life, too!"

"You're right!" said Mr. Harrison.

We got down on our knees around the hole.

"Mrs. Mentry, are you down there?" Michael hollered.

There was a long pause, and then . . .

"Of *course* I'm down here!" yelled a far-away voice. "Why is there a hole in the floor? I'm going to sue the school!"

Mrs. Mentry sounded pretty mad.

"The school is fifty years old," Mr. Harrison yelled into the hole. "Stuff is breaking all the time."

"Tell me what you see," Neil yelled. "Any dead squirrels down there?"

"I can't see *anything*!" Mrs. Mentry shouted back. "Get me out of here! I need to call my lawyer."

"Don't touch any wires, Mrs. Mentry," Andrea warned her.

Mr. Harrison looked at us seriously.

"I'm too big to fit through this hole, kids," he said. "A few of you need to go down there and help get Mrs. Mentry out."

We all wanted to go down the hole except for Emily, who was scared, of course. Mr. Harrison chose the skinniest ones—me, Andrea, Alexia, and Ryan—to go down there and rescue Mrs. Mentry.

We lowered ourselves through the hole one at a time. It was scary, but exciting, too. The candles on our cake didn't give off a lot of light.

"I'm down," I said when my

feet touched the bottom. It was dusty and dirty.

"Mrs. Mentry?" Andrea asked. "Where are you?"

Silence.

"Do you see anything?" Alexia asked.

"No."

"I've just seen a face," said Ryan.

"Where?" said Andrea. "Is it Mrs. Mentry?"

At that moment the scariest thing in the history of the world happened. I heard a deep, rumbling sound, then a crash. And the next thing I knew, the ceiling was falling on top of us!

It was a cave-in!

11

I Don't Want to Hold Your Hand

"Help!"

That was the first word I heard when I opened my eyes. I'm not sure if I was out for a few seconds or a few hours. It didn't feel like I had broken any bones or anything. There was concrete and dust and junk here, there, and everywhere.

"Am I dead?" I asked.

"I don't think so, Arlo," said Andrea. "Unless we're both dead."

I knew I couldn't be dead, because if I was in heaven, Andrea wouldn't be there.

When the dust had cleared, I was in a little cave deep beneath the ground with Andrea, Alexia, and Ryan. Luckily, the

whole school hadn't fallen on our heads. Except for a few scratches, we were all okay.

I could hardly see a thing. My candle was gone. My cake was gone too. I was cold. This was the worst thing to happen since TV Turnoff Week.

"We're trapped," Ryan said, "like those miners in Chile."

"Those miners were underground for *months* before they got rescued!" said Alexia.

"Hey, maybe we'll be on TV when we get out," I said. "The miners in Chile were on TV all the time."

"TV?" said Andrea, all excited. "How do

I look? Is my hair messed up?"

I couldn't even see Andrea's dumb hair. It was too dark.

"Will you stop thinking about how you look for once?" Alexia told her. "We could *die* in here!"

Die?

I hadn't even thought about dying until Alexia brought it up. I wished I could run away to Antarctica and go live with the penguins.

Then I heard another voice, in the distance. It was coming from far above our heads. It sounded like Mr. Harrison.

"Are you kids okay?" he yelled.

"I feel fine," yelled Andrea.

"An emergency rescue crew is coming," he hollered. "They have a giant drill. We'll have you kids out of there soon."

"Where did they get a giant drill?" I asked.

"From Rent-A-Giant Drill," Mr. Harrison said. "You can rent anything."

"What about Mrs. Mentry?" Andrea asked. "She's not with us."

"She's okay," Mr. Harrison said. "Just before the cave-in, she crawled out of the hole that Digger dug in the playground."

"I'll bet she's really mad," Ryan said. "She'll probably never visit our school again."

Mr. Harrison told us that it might take

the emergency rescue crew a few hours to drill a hole through the cement and pull us out that way. He sounded really upset.

"I should have known better," he said. "I never should have let you kids go down there."

"It's okay, Mr. Harrison," Andrea hollered up to him.

I sat on the floor between Andrea and Alexia. Ryan sat across from us. There wasn't a lot of room, so we had to sit close together.

"I'm scared," Andrea said. "What if they can't rescue us? Hold my hand, Arlo."

"I'm not holding your hand," I told her. "Hold Ryan's hand."

"I don't want to hold her hand," Ryan said.

"I want to hold *your* hand, Arlo," Andrea said.

"Don't bother me," I told her.

"Hey, I want to hold A.J.'s hand, *too*," said Alexia.

"I asked if I could hold Arlo's hand *first*," Andrea told Alexia.

"So?" Alexia said. "You get to hold his hand all the time. It's my turn to hold his hand."

"Stop fighting!" I told them. "I don't want to hold *either* of your hands."

That's when the weirdest thing in the history of the world happened. Andrea and Alexia started *crying*.

"Okay, okay," I said. "I'll hold *both* of your hands. Just stop crying."

I held hands with Andrea and Alexia. Ugh, disgusting!

"*Ooooo!* You're holding hands in the dark with two girls, A.J.," said Ryan. "You must be in *love* with them!"

"Quiet, dumbhead," I told Ryan.

I had to sit in the dark and hold hands with Andrea and Alexia for a million hundred hours. I thought I was gonna die.

"Isn't this romantic, Arlo?" Andrea asked.

"No."

"I wish we still had our candles," said Alexia.

"Candles are *so* romantic," said Andrea.

"Yeah," I said, "people must have been romantic all the time before Thomas Edison invented the lightbulb."

We were down there for a million hundred hours. It didn't seem like we were *ever* going to be rescued.

"Arlo," Andrea said. "Do you want to know a secret?"

"No."

"In case we don't make it out of here, I

want to tell you something," said Andrea, "something I've been wanting to tell you for a long time."

"I don't want to hear it."

"She loves you," said Alexia.

"That's not what I was going to say!" Andrea said. "What I wanted to say was—"

But she didn't get the chance to finish her sentence, because at that very moment we heard a loud drilling sound above us.

"They're coming to rescue us!" I shouted.

We all cheered. Finally, I could let go of the girls' hands.

The drilling got louder, and a few minutes later we saw a little hole open up above our heads. Mr. Harrison put his eyeball against the hole.

"When are you going to get us out of here?" I shouted up at him.

"Any time at all," he said. "It won't be long. I'm fixing a hole. I'll get you. I will. We can work it out. I've got a feeling. All I've got to do . . ."

Mr. Harrison wasn't making any sense at all.

"What should we do?" I asked.

"I need you," he said. "See that big rock over there? Move it over to the side so the drill can get through."

I tried to move the rock, but it was too heavy.

"I'm so tired," I groaned.

Ryan and the girls crawled over to help.

"Dig it," Mr. Harrison told us. "Carry that weight. All together now. Don't let me down."

All four of us pushed against the rock as hard as we could. Finally, with a little help from my friends, I was able to slide it out of the way.

"Okay!" Mr. Harrison said. "We're going to drill again. Wait. Get back."

We moved out of the way, and the drill started up again. It was really loud. Pieces

of cement were falling around us. It was scary and cool at the same time.

And then, suddenly, the drill came through, and we could see a big hole open above us. Light flooded in. We could hear all the kids upstairs cheering.

"Here comes the sun!" I shouted.

"We're saved!" Andrea yelled.

We were about to climb up through the hole when I heard a noise in the corner. There was movement.

"What's that?" Alexia asked.

"Maybe it's the fried squirrel," said Ryan.

"It's not a fried squirrel!" said Andrea. "It's a *live* squirrel. It's Digger!"

"EEEEEEEEEEEEEEEEEEEEEEEK!"

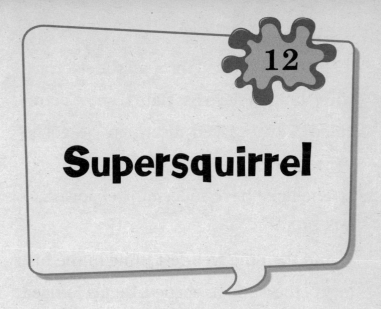

12

Supersquirrel

A live squirrel was staring at me, no more than two feet away! Ryan, Andrea, Alexia, and I climbed out of that hole in the ground like our pants were on fire. You should have been there! I thought I was gonna die!

"If Digger chewed through the electrical wire, how come she didn't get electrocuted?" Ryan asked me when we got to the top.

"She must have supersquirrel powers," I told him.

And then the weirdest thing in the history of the world happened. Digger jumped out of the hole after us! She looked all scared, like she didn't know what to do or where to go. She was sitting there looking at everybody.

"*Oooh!* Look at the cute squirrel," all the girls yelled. "It's adorable!"

"Kill it!" yelled all the boys.

We started chasing Digger down the hall. I didn't know what we were going to do if we caught her, but it was fun anyway. Finally, one of the teachers opened a door and Digger ran out of the school.

When we got back to the front office, all the lights in the school suddenly went back on again. Everybody cheered.

Ella Mentry was standing by herself in the front hallway waiting for a ride home. There was dirt on her face, and her clothes looked kind of muddy and messed up. She

didn't look very happy.

"I'll be on my way," she said when she saw us.

"I'm so glad you're okay, Mrs. Mentry," said Andrea. "Will you come back and visit us again sometime?"

"Sure," she replied, "over my dead body."

Hip hip hooray! Ella Mentry is going to come back and visit us after she's dead!

"Goodbye," we all said when a car pulled up to drive her home.

After it was over, we were on the TV news, and there was a picture in the newspaper of me being chased out of the hole by Digger the supersquirrel. It was a real Kodak moment. Kids were asking me for my autograph. I was a famous celebrity, like that Snooki lady on TV.

Maybe we'll get our own reality TV show. Maybe Ella Mentry will sue Ella Mentry School. Maybe Mr. Harrison really

is one of the Beatles. Maybe Digger will dig another hole into the school. Maybe Mr. Granite will get through page twenty-three in our math book. Maybe Mrs. Lilly will finally get a scoop so she can pick up her dog's poop. Maybe grown-ups will stop drinking so much coffee. Maybe I'll find out what Andrea wanted to say to me when we were trapped in the cave-in. Maybe we'll finally get off the fritz. Maybe we'll be able to talk Mrs. Mentry into coming back to visit our school again while she's still alive.

But it won't be easy!

the End

Within this book are hidden the titles to forty-five Beatle songs. How many of these can you find? Ask your mom or dad to help.

"Good Morning, Good Morning"
"Yesterday"
"I Want to Hold Your Hand"
"Hello Little Girl"
"Tell Me Why"
"Because"
"Birthday"
"Run for Your Life"
"No Reply"
"I Saw Her Standing There"
"You Won't See Me"
"You Can't Do That"
"Tell Me What You See"
"I'm Down"
"I've Just Seen a Face"

"Help!"
"Here, There, and Everywhere"
"I Feel Fine"
"I Should Have Known Better"
"Don't Bother Me"
"Do You Want to Know a Secret?"
"I Want to Tell You"
"Something"
"She Loves You"
"Any Time at All"
"It Won't Be Long"
"Fixing a Hole"
"I'll Get You"
"I Will"
"We Can Work It Out"
"I've Got a Feeling"

"All I've Got to Do"
"I Need You"
"I'm So Tired"
"Dig It"
"Carry That Weight"
"All Together Now"
"Don't Let Me Down"
"With a Little Help from My Friends"
"Wait"
"Get Back"
"Here Comes the Sun"
"I'll Be on My Way"
"Goodbye"
"The End"